I'VE GOT YOUR NOSE!

I'VE GOT YOUR NOSE!

NANCY BENTLEY

ILLUSTRATED BY DON MADDEN

DOUBLEDAY

NEW YORK LONDON TORONTO SYDNEY AUCKLAND

PUBLISHED BY DOUBLEDAY
a division of Bantam Doubleday Dell Publishing Group, Inc.
666 Fifth Avenue, New York, New York 10103
DOUBLEDAY
and the portrayal of an anchor with a dolphin
are trademarks of Doubleday, a division of
Bantam Doubleday Dell Publishing Group, Inc.
Library of Congress Cataloging-in-Publication Data
Bentley, Nancy.
I've got your nose! / Nancy Bentley ; illustrated by Don Madden —1st ed.
p. cm.
Summary: Unhappy with her little button nose, a witch tries to cast a spell to change it to a long pointy one with warts.
ISBN 0-385-41297-5 (pbk.)—ISBN 0-385-41296-7 (lib. bdg.)
[1. Witches—Fiction. 2. Nose—Fiction.] I. Madden, Don, 1927–ill. II. Title.
PZ7.B447497Iag 1991
[E]—dc20 90-34867 CIP AC
RL: 2.9

Designed by Diane Stevenson/SNAP·HAUS GRAPHICS

Printed in the United States of America
October 1991
First Edition

For my parents,
George and Antoinette Bentley

O.C.
SPELLS

Nahzella the witch loved many things. She loved O.C. (her old cat), and she loved her messy cottage. She loved magic spell punch and bat-wing sandwiches. But the one thing Nahzella did not love was her nose. Her nose was a cute little button fit for a princess, not for a witch.

"I want to look ugly and frightening, not cute," she said to O.C. He rubbed up against her legs. "I don't scare anyone with a nose like this!"

So Nahzella locked her cottage door, reached for her magic spell book, and looked under "N": *Nasty, Needle, Newt, Night . . .*

"Ah, here we are—*Nose,*" Nahzella cackled. Day and night she practiced her magic spells. O.C. curled up nearby.

One spell gave her a wonderful green nose with a spider on the end. That afternoon while she napped outside, an army of ants marched over her nose, thinking it was grass. O.C. hissed them away.

One spell called for a clothespin to make her nose longer, but all she got was a headache and two red spots. O.C. licked her face.

Another spell gave her a nose that glowed. But moths flew around it all night. O.C. batted them away.

"Enough of this!" she yelled. "I'll go to town and use one of my spells to steal someone *else's* nose. Any one of them must be uglier than mine!"

So she picked up her magic spell book and looked under "S": *Scary, Slimy, Snake, Sorcerer . . .*

"Ah, here we are—*Steal,*" said Nahzella as she bent over the book. She disguised herself as an old fairy godmother, stuck cutout stars on her dress, and wrapped ribbon around her broomstick to make it look like a wand. Off she went with O.C. hidden in her picnic basket.

After walking an hour in the hot sun, Nahzella sat down to rest. A farmer taking his hay to market rode by in a cart. He had a long pointy nose which he blew with a large handkerchief. Nahzella looked eagerly at his nose. Then she cast a spell:

"Fiddle-de-dee
Fiddle-de-rose
I'm going to take your long pointy
nose!"

In an instant Nahzella had the farmer's nose and the farmer had Nahzella's nose.

"Mornin', ma'am," he said politely as he tipped his hat. Taking in a deep breath with his new nose, he put his handkerchief into his overalls and rode off.

Nahzella clapped her hands with glee. "Quick, O.C., hand me my mirror. Let's see how I look!"

She gazed at the long pointy nose on her face. Just then she sneezed an enormous sneeze. Her hat fell off.

"Ah-ah-choo!" Another sneeze knocked her to the ground.

"Oh, no! That farmer has hayfever! This nose will never do!"

Sneezing away, Nahzella hurried after the farmer.

CHOOO

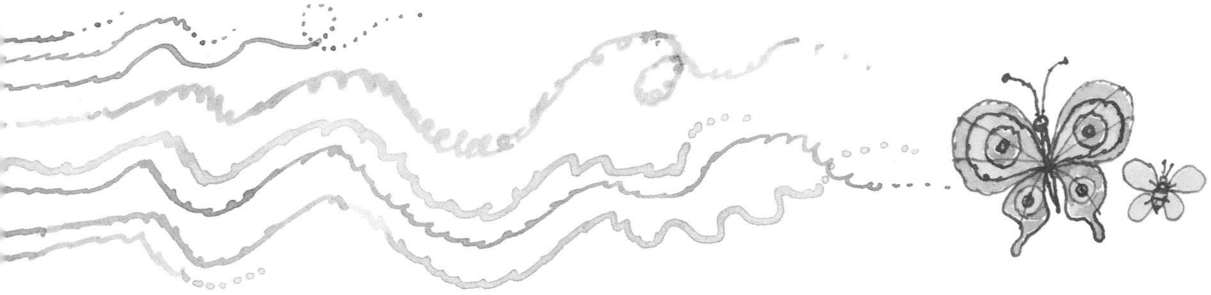

Soon a plump baker with a load of fresh bread passed by. He was on his way to market.

"Ah-ah-choo! Good morning, Mr. Baker," Nahzella said. She dabbed her nose with a handkerchief. "What wonderful loaves of bread you have."

"Why thank you, old woman," said the baker. He closed his eyes and took a deep breath of the fresh bread.

"I'd follow the scent of these loaves anywhere!" he said. Nahzella noticed that the baker's nose was big and red. That's the nose for me, she thought.

As he turned his back and started toward the town gate, Nahzella cast another spell:

"Fiddle-de-dee
Fiddle-de-rose
I'm going to take your big red nose!"

All at once, Nahzella had a brand-new nose. The baker, who now had the farmer's nose, sneezed and continued on his way. Nahzella grabbed the mirror, while O.C. stared at her.

"Oh—what a horribly perfect nose!"

Suddenly her new nose swiveled her head around and made two loud sniffs and a snort. The nose pulled her to her feet, took a deep breath, and set off toward the fragrant loaves of bread.

"Oh, no!" she cried helplessly. "Wait!"

She snatched her picnic basket in one hand and O.C.'s tail in the other. Nahzella's big red nose led her into every bakery shop in town. Her hair slipped out from under her hat. Stars tumbled from her dress.

She grabbed a lamppost and looked up and down the street.

An old butcher stood in the doorway of his shop, scratching his wrinkled nose.

"This is my chance for a better nose," said Nahzella. Wheezing feebly, she cast a third spell:

"Fiddle-de-dee
Fiddle-de-rose
I'm going to take your wrinkly old nose!"

MEATS

But this time Nahzella was so tired that her spell landed on the butcher's dog, who was asleep at his feet.

"Oh, no!" But it was too late for Nahzella. She now had a shiny black nose on her face. The dog jumped up and trotted right off for the bakery, sniffing the bread with his new nose.

"Hmmm," said Nahzella. "This nose might not be so bad after all. Black *is* my favorite color."

But before she could take out her mirror, the new nose pulled her face into her picnic basket. It sniffed at O.C. O.C. sprang out and hissed at the round black nose on Nahzella's face.

"Oh, no!" Nahzella said. "Now what have I done?" O.C. scampered up a tree.

Just then the hay farmer pulled out of the livery station. He frowned as he looked at Nahzella sniffing the ground nearby.

A little boy standing next to the cart looked down at Nahzella and started to cry.

"O.C.!" Nahzella yelled. "I've done it! I'm scary at last!" O.C. arched his back and took a swipe at her with his paw. Nahzella frantically circled the tree, her black nose sniffing away.

"O.C.!" Nahzella yelled. "It's me!" She got so befuddled and so angry that she threw her magic spell book on the ground and sputtered:

"Fiddle-de-dee
Fiddle-de-by
What did I see with
My crazy old eye?
Fiddle-de-dee
Fiddle-de-rose
Give me your terrible toes...
I mean clothes...
Oh dear, I mean ears...
Oh my, I'm going to cry..."

Nahzella slumped to the ground, but she didn't look at all like her old self. She now had the farmer's eyes, the baker's coat, the butcher's ears, and the dog's toes.

SPELLS

O.C. let out a mournful yowl.

Nahzella picked up the magic spell book and threw it high into the air. Then she shut her eyes as tightly as she could and yelled as loudly as she could:

"Fiddle-de-dee
Fiddle-de-rose
Give each one back his very own nose!
And ears... and clothes... and eyes... and toes!"

SPELLS

CHOO

There was a great explosion and a puff of smoke.

A loud sneeze knocked the farmer to the ground. He put his handkerchief to his long pointy nose and blew.

The baker closed his eyes and took a deep breath of the fresh bread with his big red nose.

The dog sniffed the air with his black nose and fell asleep.

Nahzella stood straight up and wriggled her cute little nose back and forth. With a flick of her broom she reached up to O.C., who held one paw over his nose as he jumped onto her hat. She shook off her stars and glitter, unraveled the ribbon from her broomstick, and flew home singing:

"Fiddle-de-dee
Fiddle-de-rose
The best thing for me is my very own nose!"

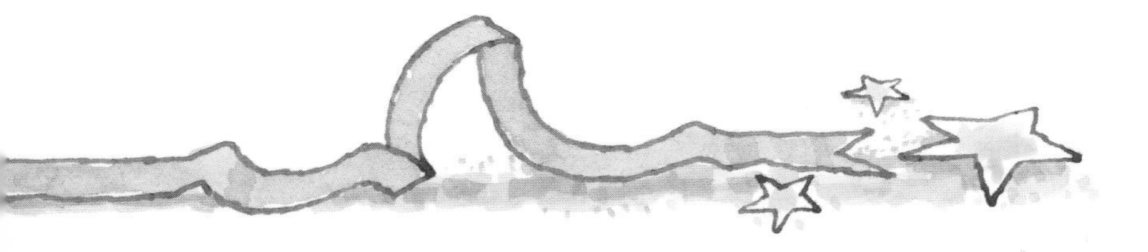